FIRST CHAPTER BOOKS

TIME CHRONICLES

READ WITH Biff, Chip & Kipper

The Matrix Mission

Written by David Hunt
and illustrated by Alex Brychta

Before reading

- Read the back cover text and page 4. What do you think the Virans will do next?
- Look at page 5. Do you think the Matrix will work differently to a computer keyboard?

After reading

- Can you find things that happened in the story that might have helped Johann to invent the printing press?

Book quiz

1 What year does Neena travel to?

   a 1411

   b 1414

   c 1428

2 Why can't anyone leave or enter the city of Mainz?

3 Where did Johann hide the Matrix?

See p45 for the book quiz answers!

The story so far ...

The Matrix is a vital part of the TimeWeb, an ancient computer that can detect where Virans are attacking the past.

While Biff and Chip wait anxiously in the Time Vault, Neena faces extreme danger.

Can she bring the Matrix safely back to Mortlock, the Time Guardian? Or will the Virans get to it first?

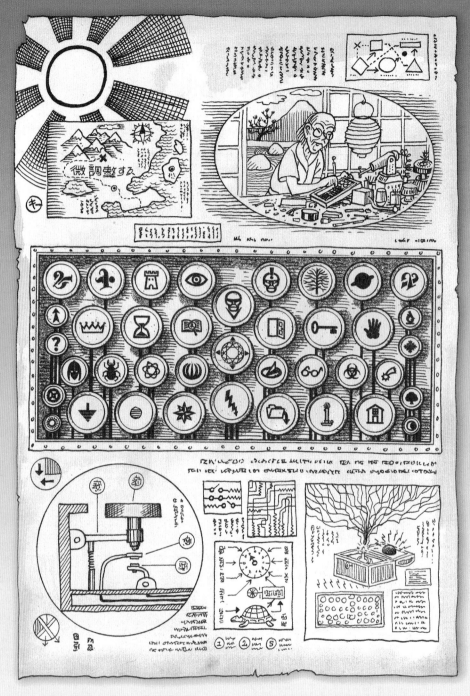

Part of the TimeWeb – the Matrix

"... the Matrix is like the keyboard of a computer ..."

Theodore Mortlock – Time Guardian

Chapter 1

Neena felt as if she was sliding down an invisible tube. Colours flashed before her eyes. Noises came and went.

Then, silence ...

She had no idea where she was. She had arrived somewhere back in time ... and she knew she was alone.

Johann's eyes strained in the candlelight. He pulled the old book he was copying closer to the flame. He had to make an accurate copy for the Archbishop.

His inky fingers brushed the page.

"Careful!" he muttered.

To make a blot would mean starting that page again. That would take hours. The Archbishop would only pay him for a perfect copy, no matter how long it took.

Suddenly, a shaft of bright light broke through the gloom. Johann narrowed his eyes. A figure had stepped into the room.

"Who are you?" gasped Johann.

"I'm Neena. Mortlock sent me," said Neena.

The name Mortlock made Johann jump. He knocked over his bottle of ink. He had not heard that name for a long time but he knew what it meant.

"You must be from the future," he said. "You look ... different from us."

The black ink spread like a dark shadow over the page of careful work. Johann's heart beat faster.

"Then you have come for the Matrix," he muttered. "I never thought the time would come."

He rose quickly to his feet. "Come with me. We've no time to lose."

Chapter 2

Neena followed Johann out of a chapel
building at the side of the Archbishop's
palace. She ran after him through rows of
grapevines to a dusty barn.

Johann pulled open the heavy wooden
door of the barn and beckoned her inside.

At the end of the barn were rows of barrels. Neena could see a girl about her own age scrubbing a large wooden machine.

"This is my sister," said Johann. "She's cleaning the wine press in time for the grape harvest."

"Elsa, this is Neena," said Johann. "She
has come for the Matrix."

"But we haven't got it!" gasped Elsa. "We
left it hidden in our father's workshop in
the city."

Neena held up her hands. "Please! Slow
down!" she said. "First, tell me where I am."

"At the Archbishop's country palace near the city of Mainz. It is 1411," said Johann.

"But the city gates are locked," said Elsa. "No one is allowed to go in or out."

Neena was puzzled. "Why?" she asked.

"A few days ago, strangers came to the city," said Elsa. "They said they had orders to shut it down. They told people to leave."

"Most people couldn't afford to leave," said Johann. "Those who could leave, did."

"What did the strangers tell everyone?" asked Neena.

Johann looked worried. "They said a plague called the Black Death was on the way, and would soon be in Mainz."

"All the gates were locked. Every bridge was guarded," went on Elsa. "Everyone who left was stopped and searched."

"Ugh!" shuddered Johann. "The man who searched us was weird. He made me feel cold even though it was a hot day."

Neena's eyes widened. "Virans!" she exclaimed. "What if those men are Virans? What if there is no plague? Could they be spreading panic so they can search the city for the Matrix?"

"If they are looking for the Matrix, they could be at Father's workshop right now," said Johann, anxiously.

"Then we must get to it before they do," said Neena. "How can we get into the city?"

"It's impossible," replied Johann.

"It may not be," said Elsa. "I have an idea."

Chapter 3

It was late in the afternoon before Johann put down his pen and folded the letter.

Neena carefully dripped red sealing wax on to the paper. Elsa had moulded the Archbishop's shield in a lump of clay. As the wax set, she pushed the shield into it.

"A letter from the Archbishop giving us permission to go into the city," she said.

Johann studied the letter. "It's a bit of a rushed job," he said. "But it'll do."

"Rushed?" laughed Neena. "It took ages! Where I come from, printing a letter takes seconds."

"What?" asked Johann, puzzled.

"Oh, it doesn't matter," smiled Neena.

With the letter finished, the children set off. Elsa had given Neena some clothes to wear. "You need to look like a servant," she told Neena.

Neena felt hot in the heavy skirt and cloak as they hurried down the valley.

Soon they reached the river. On the other side was the city. Beyond its walls were rooftops and church spires. It all looked so peaceful. The river glistened in the sun like liquid gold.

The main bridge to the city was guarded by two dark figures. They were searching a cart and questioning the driver.

Chapter 4

Some way upstream from the bridge was a paper mill. The mill was deserted, but the huge waterwheel still turned slowly.

Elsa gripped Johann's arm.

"I'll wait here at the mill," she said. "If you are not back by nightfall, I'll get help. Good luck!"

Johann and Neena were soon at the bridge.

A figure moved out in front of them.

Neena shuddered. She felt a strange coldness as the man approached.

"What is your business?" the man asked.

Johann handed him the letter. "We come on the orders of the Archbishop."

"The Archbishop?" The man looked at them suspiciously. "What does he want?"

Neena gulped.

"He wishes us to fetch an important book from the cathedral," said Johann.

"At your own risk," the man muttered. "There's a plague in this city."

Johann and Neena hurried on, but then they heard a shout. Neena glanced back to see a second man waving the letter. The two men began to charge after them.

"Come back!" one yelled.

"They've seen through us! Run, Neena," gasped Johann.

They ran down narrow streets and darted through passageways.

At last Johann stopped.

"I think we've lost them," he panted.

He opened a door leading into a courtyard, crossed the yard and climbed on to a high wall.

Neena flung off her cloak and leaped up. Johann caught her wrist and hauled her up. Then they dropped to the other side.

Chapter 5

They had reached the workshop. In front of them was a heavy door with two locks. Johann took two huge keys from his belt and unlocked the door.

"My father makes coins here," said Johann as he pushed the heavy door open.

In the workshop, tools hung on every wall. To one side was a large brick furnace.

On a bench was a tray of metal blocks. It looked rather like a computer keyboard. Neena gasped. It looked very much like the drawing she had seen of the Matrix.

She looked round anxiously. What if the Virans were to come now? "Is this it?" she asked.

"No, these are punches that make coins," said Johann. He picked one out. "You hit this on to a metal disc and stamp an imprint."

He began to dig in a bunker of charcoal, reaching to the bottom with his hands.

"What are you doing?" asked Neena. "You'll get filthy!"

"Exactly!" he said. He pulled out a metal tray. "No one would think of looking for the Matrix in here."

Even though it was black from the charcoal, the Matrix was so beautiful that they both fell silent.

It looked similar to the tray of punches, except each block had a different symbol carved into it.

"Where did it come from?" asked Neena.

"The East, I think," said Johann.

Suddenly the light from the oil lamp grew dim. An icy coldness swept over them both.

The dark figure of a Viran stood in the doorway. He was holding the cloak Neena had flung off before she climbed the wall.

"Without the Matrix, the Time Guardians will be lost," he hissed. Then he slowly held out his hand. "Give!"

Chapter 6

Johann held the Matrix behind him. He and Neena backed away. The Viran moved towards them.

Suddenly, Johann fell over a stool. He cried out in pain as he landed on the Matrix.

Neena saw her chance. "Take it!" she shouted, holding out the tray of punches.

The Viran turned towards her. Neena felt an icy chill of fear. But at that moment, Johann picked up an oil lamp and flung it at the Viran's feet.

At once the burning oil ran across the floor in a low curtain of flame.

The Viran let out a cry and sprang back.

"Run, Neena!" shouted Johann. "Run!"

Chapter 7

They raced through the city streets. When they got near the bridge they could see Virans guarding it.

"They'll soon know they've been tricked," said Johann. "We won't get out of the city."

"We'll have to cross the river another way," said Neena.

They scrambled along the bank. Moored some way upstream was a small rowing boat.

Almost at once, they found the strong current was taking them down towards the bridge. "Any closer, and the Virans will see us," said Johann urgently.

"Aim for the paper mill," shouted Neena.

More by chance than skill, Johann steered the little boat across to the mill. He slammed the boat against the side of the wall.

"Climb on to the waterwheel," he called. "Step on to one of the paddles, and hold on."

As the waterwheel turned, they were lifted up out of the river and on to a platform at the top.

Elsa was waiting for them. "You made it," she said. As she spoke, a doorway suddenly appeared. The mission was over.

Johann and Elsa watched as Neena stepped through the doorway.

"Take care of the Matrix," said Johann.

As he turned Neena noticed that on the back of his shirt, the charcoal dust had left a perfect print of the Matrix.

"You made the imprint when you fell on it in the workshop," laughed Neena.

"A print!" said Johann. "There's an idea."

But Neena had vanished.

Now what?

Was there really a plague in the city or were the Virans spreading panic, just as Neena suspected?

How did Neena and Johann outwit the Virans? Do you think the Virans will learn from their mistakes?

Did the mission help Johann to invent a printing press?

Now the Matrix is safe ... But will it be enough?

Find out by reading the following:

The Power of the Cell or

The Time Web

... Every second is precious, so hurry!

History: downloaded!
Johannes Gutenberg

Johannes Gutenberg was born around 1398 and spent his childhood in the city of Mainz, on the river Rhine. During Johannes' childhood, paper arrived in the city for the first time – it was a new invention from Asia.

Around this time, many people in Mainz caught a deadly illness called the plague. Johannes was lucky. His father worked in the city mint making coins. Because of this, the Gutenbergs were allowed to leave the city and take shelter at the Archbishop's castle.

Old map of Mainz

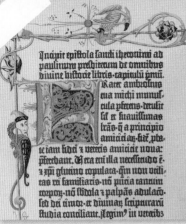

In the Archbishop's library, Johannes would have seen the scribes as they painstakingly copied out books by hand. He may even have helped.

Johannes may also have helped with the Archbishop's wine harvest. Certainly he would have watched the grapes being crushed by wine presses.

The wine presses and all the other things Johannes had seen helped to give him the idea for one of the most amazing inventions of all time: **the printing press.** Using this, books could easily be printed over and over again, and ideas could spread quickly, far and wide.

For more information, see the Time Chronicles website:
www.oxfordprimary.co.uk/timechronicles

Glossary

accurate *(page 7)* Exactly right, totally correct. *He had to make an accurate copy for the Archbishop.*

archbishop *(page 7)* Christian term for the most important bishop of a region. In this word, 'arch' means 'chief'. A chief bishop.

harvest *(page 12)* The time of year when a crop is ready to be gathered. *"She's cleaning the wine press in time for the grape harvest."*

plague *(page 15)* A deadly disease that spreads very quickly. *"They said a plague called the Black Death was on the way, and would soon be in Mainz."*

sealing wax *(page 18)* Wax used to seal a letter. A ring or stamp was pressed into melted wax on the fold of a letter. The letter could then not be opened without breaking the seal. *Neena carefully dripped red sealing wax on to the paper.*

shield *(page 18)* Here means a badge – sometimes called 'a coat of arms', to represent a family name or title such as archbishop. *Elsa had moulded the Archbishop's shield in a lump of clay.*

suspiciously *(page 24)* With a feeling that something is wrong. *The man looked at them suspiciously.*

Thesaurus: Another word for ...

accurate *(page 7)* exact, precise, correct.

Have you read them all yet?

Level 11:

Level 12:

Time Runners	Mission Victory
Tyler: His Story	The Enigma Plot
A Jack and Three Queens	The Thief Who Stole Nothing

More great fiction from Oxford Children's:

About the Authors

Roderick Hunt MBE - creator of best-loved characters Biff, Chip, Kipper, Floppy and their friends. His first published stories were those he told his two sons at bedtime. Rod lives in Oxfordshire, in a house not unlike the house in the Magic Key adventures. In 2008, Roderick received an MBE for services to education, particularly literacy.

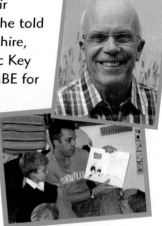

Roderick Hunt's son **David Hunt** was brought up on his father's stories and knows the world of Biff, Chip and Kipper intimately. His love of history and a good story has sparked many new ideas, resulting in the *Time Chronicles* series. David has had a successful career in the theatre, most recently working on scripts for Jude Law's *Hamlet* and *Henry V,* as well as Derek Jacobi's *Twelfth Night.*

Joint creator of the best-loved characters Biff, Chip, Kipper, Floppy and their friends, **Alex Brychta MBE** has brought each one to life with his fabulous illustrations, which are known and loved in many schools today. Following the Russian occupation of Czechoslovakia, Alex Brychta moved with his family from Prague to London. He studied graphic design and animation, before moving to the USA where he worked on animation for Sesame Street. Since then he has devoted many years of his career to *Oxford Reading Tree,* bringing detail, magic and humour to every story! In 2012 Alex received an MBE for services to children's literature.

Roderick Hunt and Alex Brychta won the prestigious Outstanding Achievement Award at the Education Resources Awards in 2009.

43

Levelling info for parents

What do the levels mean?

Read with Biff Chip & Kipper First Chapter Books have been designed by educational experts to help children develop as readers.

Each book is carefully levelled to allow children to make gradual progress and to feel confident and enjoy reading.

The Oxford Levels you will see on these books are used by teachers and are based on years of research in schools. Below is a summary of what each Oxford Level means, so that you can help your child to improve and enjoy their reading.

The books at Level 11 (Brown Book Band):

At this level, the sentence structures are becoming longer and more complex. The story plot may be more involved and there is a wider vocabulary. However, the proportion of unknown words used per paragraph/page is still carefully controlled to help build their reading stamina and allow children to read independently.

This level mostly covers characterisation through characters' actions and words rather than through description. The story may be organised in various ways, e.g. chronologically, thematically, sequentially, as relevant to the text type and subject.

The books at Level 12 (Grey Book Band):

At this level, the sentences are becoming more varied in structure and length. Though still straightforward, more inference may be required, e.g. in dialogue to work out who is speaking. Again, the story may be organised in various ways: chronologically, thematically, sequentially, etc., so that children can reflect on how the organisation helps the reader to understand the text.

The *Times Chronicles* books are also ideal for older children who feel less confident and need more practice in order to build stamina. The text is written to be age and ability appropriate, but also engaging, motivating and funny, making them a pleasure for children to read at this stage of their reading development.

OXFORD
UNIVERSITY PRESS

Great Clarendon Street, Oxford, OX2 6DP,
United Kingdom

Oxford University Press is a department of the University of Oxford.
It furthers the University's objective of excellence in research, scholarship,
and education by publishing worldwide. Oxford is a registered trade mark
of Oxford University Press in the UK and in certain other countries

Text © Roderick Hunt and David Hunt

Text written by David Hunt, based on the original characters
created by Roderick Hunt and Alex Brychta

Illustrations © Alex Brychta

The moral rights of the authors have been asserted

Database rights Oxford University Press (maker)

First published 2010
This edition published in 2014

British Library Cataloguing in Publication Data
Data available

978-0-19-273908-7

1 3 5 7 9 10 8 6 4 2

Paper used in the production of this book is a natural, recyclable product
made from wood grown in sustainable forests. The manufacturing process
conforms to the environmental regulations of the country of origin.

Printed in China

Acknowledgements: The publisher and authors would like to thank the following
for their permission to reproduce photographs and other copyright material:

P38tl Mary Evans Picture Library; **P38tr** Eric Gevaert/Shutterstock; **P38m:** Valentin
Agapov/Shutterstock; **P38bl** Steven Wright/Shutterstock; **P38br** Patrick Poendi/Shut-
terstock; **P38-39** Jakub Krechowicz/Shutterstock; **P39tl** Mary Evans Picture Library;
P39tr: Leigh Prather/Shutterstock; **P39m** Mary Evans Picture Library; **P39br** Ermes/
Shutterstock.First published 2010

Book quiz answers

1 a

2 Strangers came to Mainz and said they had orders to shut it down.

3 In a bunker of charcoal.